Jan & Mike Berenstain

Going green
isn't hard to do.
It's good for the earth
and me and you, too!

HARPER FESTIVAL
An Imprint of HarperCollins*Publishers*

The Berenstain Bears Go Green

For information address HarperCollins Publishers, 195 Broadway, New York, NY 10007.
www.harpercollinschildrens.com
Library of Congress catalog card number: 2012937019
ISBN 978-0-06-207550-5
15 16 17 18 19 SCP 10 9
❖
First Edition

Bear Country was a beautiful place to live. It had green rolling hills and wide river valleys. It had cool shady woods and bright sunny fields.

There were steep cliffs and deep canyons, roaring rapids and rushing waterfalls.

Lots of creatures lived in Bear Country besides bears. There were deer and ducks, woodchucks and weasels. There were rabbits and raccoons, possums and porcupines.

There were badgers, bats, butterflies,
bugs, and much, much more.

The Bear family loved living in Bear Country. They always tried their best to keep it beautiful. Most of the other creatures who lived there tried their best, too. But no matter how hard you try, sometimes you run into problems. And that's just what happened.

One fine morning the Bear family decided to go fishing.

"Let's go down to the creek where Grizzly Gramps keeps his boat," said Papa. "We can pack a lunch and have a picnic as we fish."

"Terrific!" they all agreed.

GRAMPS' BOAT

The family packed up their fishing gear and their lunch and went down to the creek, where they loaded into Grizzly Gramps's boat. Papa got out the oars and rowed everyone lazily along, their fishing lines out, while they ate a picnic lunch. The sun was shining, the birds were singing, and all seemed right in Bear Country.

Until . . .

"Pew!" said Sister. "What's that awful smell?"
The rest of the family sat up and sniffed.
"Yuck!" they all cried. "What is that?"

They noticed something funny floating in the water. It was a streak of dark, gunky-looking stuff. It seemed to be coming from around a bend in the creek.

"Uh-oh!" said Papa. "I know what's around that bend!"

Soon they could all see it: the Bear Country Dump!

BEAR COUNTRY
DUMP
TRASH

"Wow!" said Brother. "What a mess!"

It was indeed a mess. There were wrecked cars, old mattresses, busted TV sets, broken washing machines, and piles of trash and garbage. But the worst mess was the bunch of leaky old oil drums that someone had dumped right on the edge of the creek. Gooey, smelly, black oil was leaking into the water.

"This is a disgrace!" said Mama. She hated to see her beloved Bear Country treated this way. Mama had even been the mayor of Bear Country for a time. "This has got to be cleaned up!" she said. "We will go to the town meeting and complain."
"Yes!" said Brother.
"Go, Mama!" said Sister.
"Go! Go!" said Honey.

HONORABLE
MAYOR

At the next town meeting, the Bear family and many other bears filled the town hall. Mayor Honeypot was on the stage. He rapped on the desk with a gavel.

"Ahem!" he said. "The meeting is called to order. Is there any new business?"

Mama stood up to speak. But another bear jumped up before her.

"Mr. Mayor," he said, "I am Mr. Greenwood, and I have come to complain about the disgraceful state of the Bear Country Dump!"

Mama sat down to listen.

BEAR COUNTRY TOWN HALL
HONORABLE MAYOR
GO GREEN

"Oil is leaking from the dump into the creek," said Mr. Greenwood. "What are you going to do about it, Mr. Mayor?"

Mayor Honeypot was surprised.

"I did not know about that," he said. "We will have a cleanup of the dump right away. Will any of you here volunteer to help?"

Everyone at the meeting raised their hands. Especially Mama, Papa, and the cubs!

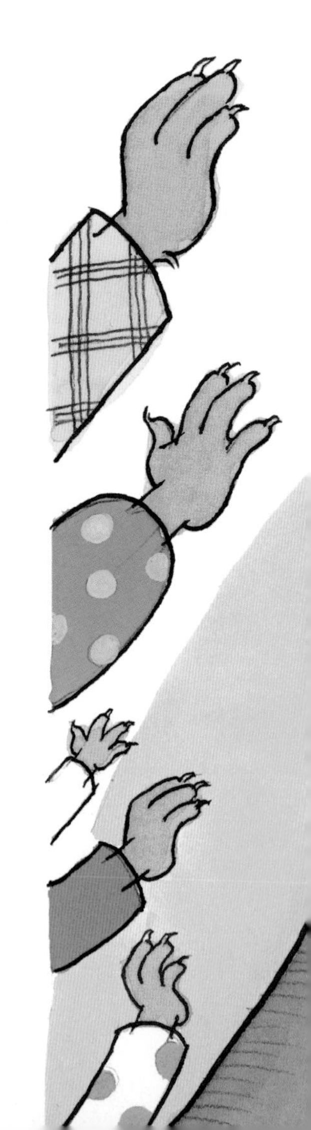

HONORABLE
MAYOR
THE
JUNK
BEARS
GRIZZLY
GUS
TRUCKING

A few days later, it seemed like most of Bear Country was down at the dump. Everyone pitched in to clean up the trash and junk. Much of it would be mixed with earth so that trees could grow on it. They hauled away the oil drums and put them in a safer spot far from the creek.

GO GREEN
JUNK BEARS

As the Bear family headed for home, Sister was thoughtful.

"You know," she said, "it's good to clean up the dump, but there's lots more we can do to make Bear Country clean and green. We can do things right at home. We've been learning about it in school."

"Like what?" asked Papa.

"Well," began Sister, "we can recycle and compost."

"We can stop wasting water and energy at home," added Brother.

"And," put in Mama, "we can carpool with other families going to school or shopping so we won't waste gas."

OFF
LOW ENERGY LIGHT
MAMA BEAR
MIZ McGRIZZ
GRIZZLY GRAN
MIZ BRUIN

But Papa had the best "going green" idea of all. He rigged up a windmill on top of his workshop to power some of his tools.

"I think wind power is the best kind of energy there is," he explained. "It's clean, it's there any windy day you want it, and best of all," he added, "it's absolutely, totally *free*!"

"Wheee!" said Honey, holding up a pinwheel to catch the wind.